LOUISA MAY ALCOTT

An Old-Fashioned Thanksgiving

Illustrated by James Bernardin

HarperCollinsPublishers

Recipe for Louisa May Alcott's Apple Slump on page 32 printed by permission of Orchard House, Concord, Massachusetts, www.louisamayalcott.org.

An Old-Fashioned Thanksgiving
Adapted text © 2005 by HarperCollins Publishers
Illustrations copyright © 2005 by James Bernardin
Manufactured in China.
www.harperchildrens.com
Library of Congress Cataloging-in-Publication Data
Alcott, Louisa May, 1832-1888.
   An old-fashioned Thanksgiving / Louisa May Alcott ; illustrated by James Bernardin.— 1st ed.
       p.   cm.
   "Recipe for Louisa May Alcott's Apple Slump on page 32."
   Summary: This adaptation of the original story follows the activities of six children in nineteenth-century New England as they prepare for the Thanksgiving holiday while Mother is away caring for Grandmother.
   ISBN 0-06-000450-9 — ISBN 0-06-000451-7 (lib. bdg.)
   [1. Family life—Fiction. 2. Thanksgiving Day—Fiction. 3. New England—Fiction.] I. Bernardin, James, ill. II. Title.
PZ7.A335Om 2005   2004022103
[E]—dc22   CIP
                                                                     AC
Typography by Jeanne L. Hogle
2 3 4 5 6 7 8 9 10
❖
First Edition

To my Yankee dad,
and all those memories
of the New England
you have shown me.
—J.B.

Many years ago, up among the New Hampshire hills,
lived Farmer Bassett and his wife, and their sons and daughters.
They were poor in money, but rich in land and love.

November had come and the crops were in. The walls of the
cheerful kitchen were hung with garlands of dried apples,
onions, and corn. Up aloft from the beams shone crookneck
squashes, juicy hams, and dried venison.

Mrs. Bassett bustled to and fro, flushed and floury, for today was Thanksgiving. Tilly, the oldest daughter, was briskly grinding spices as Prue kept time with the chopper. The twins, Roxy and Rhody, sliced away at the apples while Seth and Solomon shelled corn for popping.

"Here's a man comin' up the hill lively!" shouted Solomon, looking out the window.

It was old Mr. Chadwick, who had come to tell Mrs. Bassett that her mother was very ill, and she'd better come quickly.

"Your pa and I must go right off," said Mrs. Bassett, her head in a sad jumble of anxiety, turkey, sorrow, and haste. "I'm dreadfully sorry about Thanksgiving dinner, my dears."

The children ran about, getting their mother and father ready for the long drive.

By the time Mr. Bassett drove the old green sleigh to the door, Mrs. Bassett was waiting.

"Tilly, have the baked beans and pudding for dinner. I shall come back the minute I can. Pa will come back this afternoon, so keep snug and be good."

"Yes'm, yes'm—good-bye, good-bye!" called the children as Mr. and Mrs. Bassett drove away.

As soon as they were out of sight, Tilly rolled up her sleeves. "Now, about Thanksgiving dinner," she began.

"Ma doesn't expect us to have a real Thanksgiving dinner," said Prue. "We don't know how to make it."

"I'm sure I can roast a turkey and make a pudding as well as anybody. The pies are all ready, and if we can't boil vegetables, we don't deserve any dinner!" cried Tilly.

"Did you ever roast a turkey?" asked Roxy.

"Should you dare to try?" said Rhody, in an awestruck tone.

"Don't you want to have roast turkey, pudding, and apple slump for dinner?" The children all gazed at Tilly with round eyes, nodding hopefully. "Then all you have to do is keep out of the way, and let Prue and me work," said Tilly firmly.

Happily banished from the kitchen, the younger children gathered up their mittens and overcoats and headed to the old mill to go sledding in the crisp new snow.

Tilly and Prue put on their largest aprons and set out all the spoons, dishes, pots, and pans they could find.

"Now, we'll have dinner at five. Pa will be back by that time, and he'll be surprised to find us all ready with a Thanksgiving feast," said Tilly.

As she attacked the plum pudding, Tilly felt sure that it would turn out right, for she had seen her mother do it many times. But she forgot both sugar and salt, and she tied the pudding in the cloth so tightly that it had no room to swell. Happily unaware of these mistakes, Tilly popped the pudding into the pot.

"I can't remember what flavoring Ma puts in the stuffing," she said next. "It's either sweet marjoram or summer savory. We'll put both in, and then we are sure to be right. Prue, run and get some from the garret, while I mash the bread."

Away trotted Prue, but the garret was dark, and in her haste she got catnip and wormwood.

"It doesn't smell right, but I suppose it will when it is cooked," said Tilly. She filled the turkey with the stuffing, sewed it up, and set it to roast over the fire.

Soon all was cooking, and the girls set the table. With red-and-white china, pewter platters, and mugs and spoons to match, it looked properly dressed for the occasion.

The younger children trooped in just in time, hungry from their day of playing outdoors.

"Doesn't it look nice?" said Prue. As they admired the festive table, Tilly sniffed the air and ran over to the fireplace.

"My sakes alive!" cried Tilly. "The turkey is burned on one side, and the kettles have boiled over!"

They were just struggling to get the turkey out of the fire when Roxy called, "Here's Pa!"

"There's folks with him," added Rhody, "two big sleighs chock-full!"

In came Pa, Ma, aunt, uncle, and cousins—and even Grandma, all in great spirits, and all very surprised to find such a festive feast.

"Hurrah! Grandma's here!" cried Prue.

"It was all a mistake of old Mr. Chadwick's. He got the message wrong. Grandma was sitting up, as cheery as you please," said Mrs. Bassett.

"Your pa fetched us all up to spend the evening, and we are going to have a jolly time of it, to judge by the look of things," said Aunt Cinthy.

They all sat down to enjoy the meal, and Mrs. Bassett praised Tilly and Prue for their hard work.

But when the eating began, their pride got a fall, for Mrs. Bassett nearly choked when she tasted the stuffing.

"Tilly Bassett, whatever made you put wormwood and catnip in your stuffing?" demanded Mrs. Bassett, trying not to be severe, for all the rest were laughing, and Tilly looked ready to cry.

"It didn't do a mite of harm, for the turkey is delicious," declared Pa.

"All the vegetables are well done, and the dinner a credit to you, my dears," declared Aunt Cinthy, with a mouth full of food.

The plum pudding turned out heavy as lead and as hard as a cannonball. But it was speedily whisked out of sight, and everyone announced that the apple slump was perfect.

After the table was cleared, Uncle Mose struck up his fiddle, and everyone fell into place for a dance. All down the long kitchen they danced, and even Grandma joined in the fun.

Apples and cider finished the evening, and after hugs and kisses all around, the guests drove away in the clear moonlight.

As they watched the sleighs disappear, Mrs. Bassett gathered her family around.

"Children, we have special cause to be thankful on this day. Grandma is well, our dinner was plentiful, and we are all together," she said.

When the good-nights were over and the children in bed, silence
reigned, broken only by an occasional snore from the boys and
the soft scurry of mice in the buttery, taking their part in
this old-fashioned Thanksgiving.

Louisa May Alcott's Apple Slump

Makes 6 servings.

WHAT YOU NEED:

4 to 6 tart apples (3 cups sliced)

½ cup firmly packed brown sugar

¼ teaspoon nutmeg

¼ teaspoon cinnamon

¼ teaspoon salt

1½ cups flour

2 teaspoons baking powder

½ teaspoon salt

½ cup sugar

1 egg (well beaten)

½ cup milk

½ cup melted butter

WHAT TO DO:

1. Pare, core, and slice the apples.
2. Preheat oven to 350°. Grease the inside of a 1½-quart baking dish with butter.
3. Put the sliced apples into the dish. In a small bowl, mix the brown sugar, nutmeg, cinnamon, and 1/4 teaspoon salt. Sprinkle the mixture over the apples and stir to mix.
4. Bake apples uncovered until they are soft, about 20 minutes.
5. While the apples are baking, sift together into a bowl the flour, baking powder, ½ teaspoon salt, and sugar. Mix into this the beaten egg, milk, and melted butter. Stir gently.
6. Spread this mixture over the apples and continue baking until the top is brown and crusty (about 25 minutes).
7. Serve with whipped cream.